DIVE INTO READING!

The Garden

Henry   Lily   Mei   Pablo   Padma

DISCARD

by Gwendolyn Hooks

illustrated by Shirley Ng-Benitez

Lee & Low Books Inc.   New York

To Jo Duncan, community gardener, and Ray Ridlen, agriculturist/
horticulturist, for sharing your vast gardening expertise—G.H.

With love to Ralph, who grows a magnificent garden
and shares his veggies with us each year.—S.N-B.

Text copyright © 2018 by Lee & Low Books Inc.
Illustrations copyright © 2018 by Shirley Ng-Benitez
All rights reserved. No part of this book may be reproduced, transmitted, or stored in an
information retrieval system in any form or by any means, electronic, mechanical, photocopying,
recording, or otherwise, without written permission from the publisher.
LEE & LOW BOOKS Inc., 95 Madison Avenue, New York, NY 10016
leeandlow.com
Book design by Maria Mercado
Book production by The Kids at Our House
The illustrations are rendered in watercolor and altered digitally
Manufactured in China by Imago
Printed on paper from responsible sources
(hc) 10 9 8 7 6 5 4 3 2
(pb) 10 9 8 7 6 5 4 3 2
First Edition
Library of Congress Cataloging-in-Publication Data
Names: Hooks, Gwendolyn, author. | Ng-Benitez, Shirley, illustrator.
Title: The garden / by Gwendolyn Hooks; illustrated by Shirley Ng-Benitez.
Description: First edition. | New York: Lee & Low Books Inc., [2018] |
Series: [Dive into reading; 6] | Summary: When Lily invites her friends
to volunteer at the community garden, they learn how to dig, plant seeds,
and patiently wait for their plants to grow. Includes instructions for
growing snap peas at home.
Identifiers: LCCN 2017035216| ISBN 9781620145654 (hardcover: alk. paper)
ISBN 9781620145661 (pbk.: alk. paper)
Subjects: | CYAC: Community gardens–Fiction. | Gardening–Fiction.
Friendship–Fiction.
Classification: LCC PZ7.H76635 Gar 2018 | DDC [E]–dc23
LC record available at https://lccn.loc.gov/2017035216

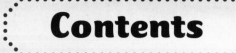

Contents

Helping   4

Planting   12

Growing   24

Helping

"I miss the garden
from our old home," said Lily.

"I miss it too," said Lily's mom.
"Let's go to the public garden.
It is a garden for everyone."

At the public garden
Lily saw her neighbor.
"Hi, Mr. Sam," said Lily.
"Do you need help?"

"Yes, I need lots of help,"
said Mr. Sam.
"I can help," said Lily.
"Maybe my friends
can help too."

At home, Lily saw her friends
Pablo, Mei, Padma, and Henry.
"Mr. Sam needs help with the
garden," Lily said.
"Do you want to help?"

"Will there be worms?"
asked Padma.
"Is it a lot of work?"
asked Henry.

"I like worms," said Mei.
"I want to help," said Pablo.
Then Padma and Henry
wanted to help too.

Lily liked planting the garden
at her old home.
But would her friends think
it was fun to garden?

Planting

Mr. Sam was happy to see Lily and her friends.
"Let's get to work," said Mr. Sam.

"Work," said Henry. "Oh no."
"It will be fun," said Lily.

"First we need to pick
seeds to plant," said Mr. Sam.
"I want to plant strawberries,"
said Pablo.
"I want to plant carrots,"
said Mei.

"I want to plant tomatoes,"
said Henry.
"I want to plant peas,"
said Padma.
"I want to plant peppers,"
said Lily.

"Next we need to find a spot
in the sun for each plant,"
said Mr. Sam.
Lily helped her friends find
a spot in the sun for each plant.

"Then we have to dig small holes
in the soil," said Mr. Sam.
Lily helped her friends dig
small holes in the soil.

"Now we need to put the seeds
in the holes," said Mr. Sam.
Lily helped her friends put
the seeds in the holes.

"Next we need to cover the seeds and water the soil," said Mr. Sam. Lily helped her friends cover the seeds and water the soil.

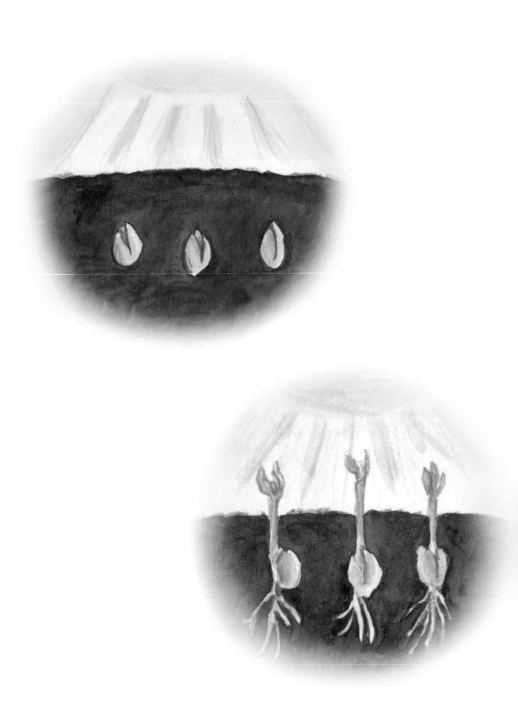

"What happens next?" asked Pablo.

"We have to wait
for the seeds to grow,"
said Mr. Sam.
"The roots and stems will grow.
Then the leaves will grow."

"When will we see our plants?" asked Padma.

"In a few months," said Mr. Sam.

"Months!" said Padma. "Oh no."
"Plants need time to grow,"
said Mr. Sam.
"Just like you."

Growing

Lily was sure her friends didn't like to garden.
But every day her friends went to the public garden with her.

They pulled weeds.
They watered the soil.
They waited and waited.

Slowly, the seeds began to grow.

The stems grew.
The leaves grew.

The plants grew and grew.
"Look at my strawberries!"
said Pablo.

"Look at my carrots!"
said Mei.
"Look at my tomatoes!"
said Henry.

"Look at my peas!" said Padma.
"And my peppers!" said Lily.
Lily also looked at her friends.
They were having fun.

"Mr. Sam, can we help you garden
next year?" asked Lily.
"Please?" asked everyone.

☆ **Activity** ☆

Would you like to plant a vegetable? Try snap peas! You can eat the peas raw or cooked.

1. You will need a container such as a milk carton or a plastic yogurt cup.

2. With the help of an adult, punch holes in the bottom of the container. This is to make sure water does not rot the roots.

3. Add soil to the container.

4. Plant one snap pea seed about an inch deep.

5. Place the container on a plastic lid or dish to catch the water.

6. Place your container in a window that gets the best sunlight.

7. Water the soil, but not too much.

8. Watch your plant grow.

9. Enjoy your peas!